FALKIRK COUNCIL LIBRARIES

D0540772

CANCELLED

Usborne

Illustrated
Stories
for
Christmas

Usborne
Illustrated
Stories
for
Christmas

CONTENTS

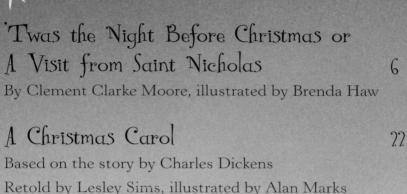

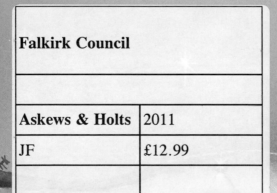

Falkirk Council	
Askews & Holts	2011
JF	£12.99

6

'Twas the Night Before Christmas

or

A Visit from Saint Nicholas

'Twas the night before Christmas,
when all through the house
Not a creature was stirring,
not even a mouse;
The stockings were hung
by the chimney with care,
In hopes that Saint Nicholas
soon would be there;

The children were nestled
all snug in their beds,
While visions of sugar-plums
danced in their heads;

And Mama in her 'kerchief,
and I in my cap,
Had just settled down
for a long winter's nap –

When out on the lawn
there arose such a clatter,
I sprang from the bed
to see what was the matter.
Away to the window
I flew like a flash,
Tore open the shutters
and threw up the sash.

11

The moon on the breast
of the new-fallen snow
Gave the lustre of mid-day
to objects below;
When, what to my wondering
eyes should appear,
But a miniature sleigh,
and eight tiny reindeer,
With a little old driver,
so lively and quick,
I knew in a moment
it must be Saint Nick.

'Twas the Night Before Christmas

More rapid than eagles
his coursers they came,
And he whistled, and shouted,
and called them by name:

"Now, Dasher! now, Dancer!
now, Prancer! now, Vixen!
On! Comet, on! Cupid,
on! Donder and Blitzen —

To the top of the porch!
to the top of the wall!
Now dash away! dash away!
dash away all!"

As dry leaves that before
the wild hurricane fly,
When they meet with an obstacle,
mount to the sky,
So up to the house-top
the coursers they flew,
With the sleigh full of toys,
and Saint Nicholas too.
And then, in a twinkling,
I heard on the roof
The prancing and pawing
of each little hoof.

As I drew in my head,
and was turning around,
Down the chimney
Saint Nicholas came with a bound.

He was dressed all in fur,
from his head to his foot,
And his clothes were all tarnished
with ashes and soot;
A bundle of toys
he had flung on his back,
And he looked like a pedlar
just opening his pack.
His eyes – how they twinkled!
his dimples how merry!
His cheeks were like roses,
his nose like a cherry!

His droll little mouth
was drawn up like a bow,
And the beard of his chin
was as white as the snow;
The stump of a pipe
he held tight in his teeth,
And the smoke it encircled
his head like a wreath;
He had a broad face
and a little round belly
That shook, when he laughed,
like a bowlful of jelly.

He was chubby and plump,
a right jolly old elf,
And I laughed when I saw him,
in spite of myself;
A wink of his eye
and a twist of his head,
Soon gave me to know
I had nothing to dread.

He spoke not a word,
but went straight to his work,
And filled all the stockings;
then turned with a jerk,
And laying his finger
aside of his nose,
And giving a nod,
up the chimney he rose.

He sprang to his sleigh,
to his team gave a whistle,
And away they all flew
like the down of a thistle;
But I heard him exclaim,
ere he drove out of sight,

"HAPPY CHRISTMAS TO ALL,
AND TO ALL A GOOD-NIGHT!"

A Christmas Carol

Marley was dead, as dead as a doornail. There was no doubt whatever about that. All that remained of the firm of *Scrooge and Marley* was Ebenezer Scrooge.

Scrooge... a grasping, greedy, gruesome old man! He was as hard as stone, and so cold inside his face looked frozen.

24

Scrooge didn't care for anyone and
hardly anyone cared for him. Even Christmas
cheer couldn't thaw his icy heart.

One Christmas Eve, he was busy in his
counting house. He had left his office door
open to keep an eye on his clerk, Bob Cratchit.

"A Merry Christmas, Uncle!" cried a cheerful voice suddenly. It was Scrooge's nephew, Fred.

"Bah, humbug!" snapped Scrooge.

What right have you to be merry? You're poor!

"If I had my way," Scrooge added, "every idiot who said 'Merry Christmas' would be cooked with his own cake!"

"Really, Uncle!" said Fred. "Come, why not eat with us tomorrow?"

"Good afternoon!" Scrooge replied, returning to his books.

As Fred left, two other men came in, collecting for the poor.

"Are there no prisons?" asked Scrooge. "No workhouses? I pay for the poor to go there. That's enough."

The men went out into the bitterly cold afternoon, shaking their heads. A little later, a scruffy carol singer paused by Scrooge's office and began to sing.

"God bless you, merry gentlemen..."

But one look at Scrooge and he fled without finishing the verse.

Finally, it was time to go home.

"You'll want the whole day off tomorrow,
I suppose?" Scrooge snarled at Bob.

"If it's convenient," said Bob.

"It isn't. Be here all the earlier the day after."

Scrooge left the office with a growl. Bob quickly locked up and set off for home. Scrooge went for his usual lonely dinner in a lonely inn.

Then he too set off for home, a few gloomy rooms in an old house which once belonged to Marley.

Now, the door knocker on this house was
not unusual, just large. And Scrooge was not
a man given to fancies. But, as Scrooge put
his key in the door, somehow he saw in the
knocker... Marley's face.

Startled, Scrooge turned the key and went in, pausing to check the back of the door as he closed it. Was the back of Marley's head sticking out into the hall? No, he saw only the lock and some screws.

"Pah, humbug!" he said, closing the door with a bang. But he checked all his rooms, just in case, before he got ready for bed.

Without warning, an old bell began to ring. It started quietly but soon rang loudly, along with every other bell in the house. Suddenly, the bells stopped. A clanking noise followed, as if someone in the cellar was dragging a heavy chain.

Then, slowly, something came through the door...

Marley's ghost?
It can't be!

Scrooge could not believe it.
"Why don't you believe your
eyes?" asked the ghost.
"Because even an upset stomach
can disturb the senses," Scrooge told him.
"Maybe the milk was sour and it's giving me
a nightmare."
The ghost let out a frightful cry and
rattled its chains.

"Mercy!" cried Scrooge. "Why do you trouble me?" Again, the ghost shook its chains. "And why are you chained up?" Scrooge added.

"These chains are a punishment for my selfish life," said the ghost. "There are some waiting for you, too, and getting heavier every day."

But you were so good at business!

My business should have been taking care of others.

"I've come here tonight to warn you,"
said the ghost. "You might escape my fate."
Scrooge looked relieved.
"You will be haunted by three spirits,"
the ghost went on.
"I think I'd rather not,"
said Scrooge.
The ghost ignored him and
headed for the window.

Expect the first
spirit when the
clock chimes one.

Scrooge closed the window and checked his door. It was still locked. "Humb—" he began, but the word stuck in his throat.

Worn out – partly from shock, partly because it was two in the morning – Scrooge fell into bed.

He was asleep in an instant.

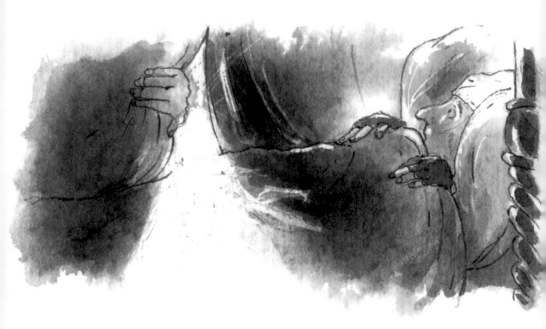

Scrooge awoke in total darkness. To his surprise, a clock chimed twelve. Twelve! But it was past two when he went to bed. "The clock's wrong," he thought. "An icicle must have got into the works."

He lay awake, fearfully counting down the next hour. On the stroke of one, a hand drew back the curtain around his bed...

Scrooge gasped. He was face to face with the strangest creature he had ever seen. A light shone out of its head and it carried a cap like a candle snuffer.

"Are you the spirit I was told about?" he asked.

"I am!" said the ghost, softly. "I'm the Ghost of Christmas Past... your past. Rise and walk with me."

Scrooge clung to the spirit as he floated through the window and out... not into the foggy city but a bright, cold day in the country.

"I was a boy here," Scrooge cried. The ghost took him to his old schoolroom where a lonely boy sat alone. "There I am," Scrooge added, sadly.

I wish I had given that carol boy something...

Before he knew it, they were back in a busy city and entering a warehouse, where a party was in full swing.

"And here I was an apprentice!" cried Scrooge. "There's my master, old Fezziwig. He made us so happy..."

Oh, why didn't I wish Bob a "Merry Christmas"?

The party faded, leaving Scrooge and the spirit outside. There was Scrooge again, now a young man, sitting beside a beautiful girl.

"I cannot marry you," she said, sadly. "You love money more than you love me."

Spirit! Show me no more...

One shadow more. Watch!

The scene changed and Scrooge found himself in a comfy room, filled with children. His old love was married to another man.

Spirit, remove me! I cannot bear it.

Scrooge began to struggle with the ghost. As he did, he noticed the light on its head burning even more brightly. Scrooge grabbed the spirit's cap and put it over the light, pressing hard.

The spirit sank down and Scrooge sank into a deep sleep.

Scrooge woke up, back in bed, as a clock struck one. He sat up nervously but nothing happened. He flung back his curtains. No one was there.

He looked around. This time he wished to challenge the spirit the moment it appeared. But still nothing happened, except for a light shining under his door

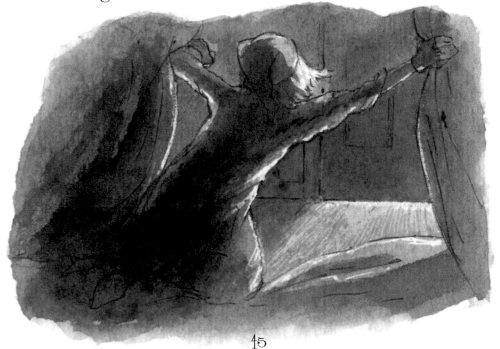

Finally, Scrooge got up and went into the next room. He could hardly recognize it. And right in the middle sat the second spirit.

Come in and know me better! I am the Ghost of Christmas Present.

Scrooge followed the ghost, through streets full of people preparing for Christmas. Finally, they came to Bob Cratchit's house, where Mrs. Cratchit was getting the Christmas dinner ready.

Where are your father and Tiny Tim?

"Here's Father!"
cried the two
youngest, as Bob
came in, carrying
his invalid son.

Soon, everyone was enjoying the feast. It
was a very small meal for such a large family
but no one would have dreamed of saying so.

A Merry Christmas
to us all!

God bless us,
every one!

"Spirit," said Scrooge suddenly, "tell me if Tiny Tim will live."

"I see an empty seat," said the ghost. "If things stay as they are, he will die."

Scrooge felt terrible, but then he heard his name.

"To Mr. Scrooge, who provided our feast!" cried Bob.

"Provided our feast, indeed!" snorted his wife. "I wish he was here. I'd give him a piece of my mind to feast upon."

By now, it was getting dark. The ghost
led Scrooge back outside, into the bustling
streets. They flew to quieter, emptier
places... but everywhere Scrooge saw people
full of Christmas spirit.

In the midst of the gloom, Scrooge heard a hearty laugh. It was his nephew Fred. They had arrived in the middle of Fred's Christmas dinner party.

He said Christmas was humbug? Shame on him!

"I feel sorry for Scrooge," said Fred. "Now, how about a game of blind man's buff?"

One game followed another. Scrooge grew so excited, he decided to join in, though no one could see or hear him.

Scrooge wanted to stay until the last guest left, but the ghost said no. "Just one more game then," Scrooge pleaded. "It's a new one called 'Yes and No'."

Is it an
animal?

Yes!

Does it
live in the
country?

No!

Does it
growl?

Yes!

Shame
on him!

Yes!

I know! It's
your Uncle
Scrooooooooge!

Yes!

"Scrooge it is!" cried Fred. "And I wish him a Merry Christmas, whatever he is."

Before Scrooge could wish Fred the same, the ghost had whisked him away. They went all over the world, finding rejoicing and hope. But the ghost was growing old.

"My life is brief," the spirit explained. "It ends at midnight."

Already the clock was chiming three quarters past eleven.

"Forgive me for asking," said Scrooge, "but is something hidden in your robes?"

"Look," the ghost replied, revealing two miserable children. "The boy is Ignorance, the girl is Want. Beware of them both, but especially the boy!"

"Have they nowhere to go?" asked Scrooge.

"Are there no prisons? No workhouses?" the spirit replied, echoing Scrooge's own words from that afternoon.

The clock struck twelve and the spirit vanished. As the last chime died away, Scrooge saw a hooded phantom coming closer...

The phantom floated slowly and silently up to Scrooge.

"Are you the Ghost of Christmas Yet To Come?" he asked.

The phantom said nothing, but pointed its ghostly hand.

"Ghost of the future," cried Scrooge, "I fear you more than any other, but I shall go with you."

Staying silent, the ghost glided off. As Scrooge followed, a city seemed to spring up around them.

I only know he's dead.

I wonder who he left his money to?

He had no friends.

They left the crowds and went to a part of town Scrooge had never visited. As they entered a junk store, three people came in with things to sell.

See — his bed curtains!
I took 'em down while he
was lying there.

I've his
boots.

Scrooge was horrified. These things had
been stolen from a dead man's house.

"Spirit, I see!" he cried. "This poor man
might be me."

As he spoke, the scene changed. Now, they were in a bedroom. A dead man lay on the bed, alone but for a cat and some rats.

The phantom pointed to the man's face, but Scrooge couldn't look.

"Is no one moved by this man's death?" he begged.

The phantom spread out his dark robe for a second. When he drew it back, Scrooge saw a room where a man and wife were talking.

"We owe him so much money," the woman said. "It would take a miracle to soften his heart."

"It's past softening," replied her husband, cheerfully. "He's dead!"

"But they are happy!" said Scrooge.
"Let me see some sorrow for a death,
spirit, please."

The phantom took him to the Cratchits'
house. Mrs. Cratchit and her children were
gathered by the fire. An air of sadness hung
over them.

As Scrooge watched them, he had the feeling that the phantom was about to leave him.

"Before you go, tell me, who was the man on the bed?" he begged.

The phantom said nothing but took
Scrooge to a churchyard.

"He lies here?" said Scrooge. Silently, the
ghost pointed to a gravestone.

"Answer me one
question, then," asked
Scrooge. "Have I seen what
will happen or what might happen?"
Still the ghost remained silent.

Trembling all over, Scrooge crept up to the gravestone and read the name upon it.

EBENEZER SCROOGE

With a terrible cry, Scrooge grabbed the ghost's robe. "No, spirit. Oh no!"

But the phantom simply pointed to Scrooge and back to the grave.

"I'm not the man I was," Scrooge cried. "Let me change."

Clinging onto the ghost, Scrooge closed his eyes to pray. When he opened them again, the phantom had become his bedpost.

He was back in his own bed.

"Ha!" he laughed. "I am as light as a feather, as happy as an angel, as merry as a school boy. Thank you, Marley! Thank you. From now on, I'll keep Christmas in my heart all year round."

"I don't know how long I was with the spirits," he babbled. "I don't know what day of the month it is. What's more, I don't care!"

Just then, the church bells rang out. Scrooge raced to his window.

What's today, boy?

Today? Why, Christmas Day!

The spirits had done all their work in one night.

Scrooge chuckled and sent the boy off to buy the butcher's prize turkey. "I'll send it to Bob Cratchit," he said to himself and rubbed his hands with glee. "It's twice the size of Tiny Tim!"

When the boy returned with the turkey, Scrooge gasped. The bird was huge. "Will you deliver it for me?" he asked, chuckling some more. "You'll need a cab."

And he paid the boy, found a cab and went back inside, still chuckling. He chuckled until the tears rolled down his cheeks.

At last, he was dressed in his best
and outside. He looked so cheerful that
several people said, "Morning sir! Merry
Christmas!" Scrooge thought those the most
beautiful words he had ever heard.

He hadn't gone far when he met the men
who had been collecting for the poor the
day before.

"Merry Christmas!" he cried. The two
men looked shocked. Was this Scrooge?

Forgive me for being so
rude yesterday.

Feeling better, Scrooge went to church and then for a walk. He had never felt so happy.

In the afternoon, he went to his nephew Fred's house. He went up to the door a dozen times before he dared knock.

Fred welcomed him to the party with such delight, Scrooge felt at home in five minutes.

It was a wonderful party. But Scrooge was at work early the next day. He wanted to catch Bob Cratchit coming in late. And he did. Bob was nearly twenty minutes late.

And just what do you mean by this?

Scrooge pretended to be furious. "I'm not going to stand for it any longer! Step into my office."

"It's only once a year," said Bob.

"I'll tell you what I'm going to do," Scrooge went on, poking him in the ribs, "I'm going to raise your salary. Merry Christmas, Bob! Now, put some more coal on the fire before you pick up your quill!"

I, er, are you sure? Oh!

Scrooge promised to take care of Bob and his family, and he was as good as his word. To Tiny Tim – who did not die – he was a second father. Not only that, he became a good friend to all who lived in his town.

Some people laughed to see the change in him. Scrooge just let them laugh. He didn't care. He knew laughing was good for them and his own heart laughed with them.

Hello Scrooge!
Hello Tim.
Lovely day!

He never saw the spirits again but it was always said of him that he knew how to have a jolly Christmas. May that be true of all of us. And so, in the words of Tiny Tim, "God bless us, every one!"

The Elf and the Toymaker

If you were to travel to the very top of the world, you would find the snowy North Pole. Some people say it's the most magical place on Earth.

For it's here, hidden away, that Santa has his toy factory. Every December, the whole place buzzes with frantic activity.

One year, it was especially busy. Santa was touring the factory, making sure everything was going to plan.

As usual, his team of tiny elves was hard at work. Each elf had a different job.

Dennis opened the letters sent by boys and girls.

Babs checked whether they'd been good or bad.

Marco read what the good children wanted for Christmas.

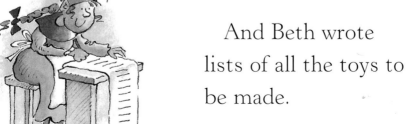

And Beth wrote lists of all the toys to be made.

87

Paddy and Pip were busy operating the toymaker. Paddy read out the name of a toy.

Pip typed it into a computer.

One robot for John.

Whiirrr!

The toymaker built it...

wrapped it...

and stuck on a label.

Alfie was sweeping the store room. He had the most boring job in the factory. It was so boring, he often... fell... aslee...

Zzzzzzzzzzz!

"Wake up, Alfie!" boomed Santa. "It's time to go home."

"Already?" yawned Alfie.

"You're always asleep on the job," complained Santa.

"Go home," he ordered, "and don't come back tomorrow unless you're wide awake."

It's not fair.

Alfie trudged through the deserted factory. "If I was in charge of the toymaker, I'd never be bored," he sighed.

Alfie had often wanted a closer look at the mysterious machine. Now was his chance.

Climbing on top, he peered down the long tube that led to the heart of the toymaker.

Wooaaah!

But he lost his balance...

and fell in!

Aghh!

Hours later, Alfie awoke surrounded by cogs and wires. His head was spinning.

"I must have knocked myself out," he thought.

Suddenly, Alfie felt the walls shake. Paddy and Pip had started up the machine.

"Oh no!" yelled Alfie. "I'll be squished into a trillion pieces."

Alfie scrambled around in panic, trying to get out. But the more he wriggled, the more he got tangled in the wiring.

"Help!" he cried desperately.

Alfie's wriggling had an odd effect on the toymaker. The first few toys came out fine...

Splendid work.

But the next batch
looked stranger...

What?

and stranger...

How?

and
stranger...

Who?

until...

Alfie?!

The toymaker began churning out hundreds of little Alfie dolls. Santa tried to turn it off, but it just kept going.

Wah!

Ouch!

Oof!

Wooaaah!

With an enormous burp, the machine shot out the real elf. Alfie came down to earth with a bump.

Santa glared at him. "The toymaker will take weeks to fix and there are still hundreds of toys to make."

"I'm s..s..sorry," sniffed Alfie.

"I'll have to give these strange little Alfie dolls instead," said Santa sadly.

But guess what? They turned out to be the most popular toy ever! Next year, Santa had requests for thousands more.

So the elves fixed the toymaker to make Alfie dolls, and Santa put Alfie in charge – as long as he stayed on the outside this time.

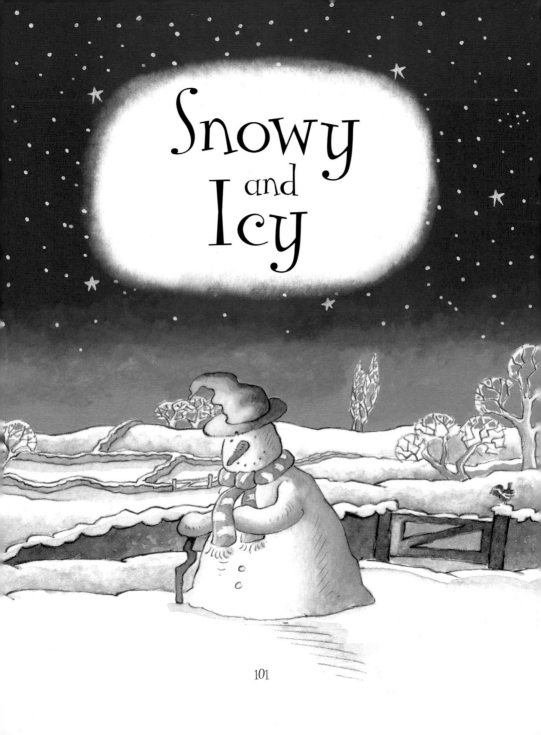

Snowy and Icy

Early one chilly morning, the children of Frostly were hard at work. Tomorrow, Christmas Eve, was judging day in the town's Best Snowman Contest.

On every street, snowmen of all shapes and sizes were being brought to life. Everyone was hoping that their creation would win first prize.

Emma Humble was putting the finishing touches to her snowman, Snowy.

He had a battered felt hat...

tiny stones for his eyes and mouth...

a moth-eaten woolly scarf...

and a broken old walking stick.

Daphne Dosh lived in a big mansion next door. She was so enormously rich, she had servants to build her snowman, Icy.

He had a shiny top hat...

sparkly buttons for his eyes and mouth...

a spotted silk scarf...

and a silver-topped cane.

Daphne peered over the fence at Emma. "Icy is twice as nice as your shabby old Snowy," she boasted, snootily.

"At least I built him myself," said Emma.

"Ha," scoffed Daphne. "That won't make any difference. Just wait and see who's the best snowman tomorrow."

That night, the snowmen of Frostly came to life.

Icy pointed at Snowy. "What a frightful sight," he jeered. "You won't win the contest."

Snowy looked at his tattered clothes with his stony eyes.

"Maybe I can make myself look better," he
said, hopefully. He set off across the fields.
Icy was certain he'd be the best snowman
in town. But he followed Snowy, just to
make sure.

Snowy saw some sheep's wool caught on a wire fence. "I could use that to patch up my scarf," he said to himself.

Icy crept up behind Snowy.

"We'll see how good your scarf looks after it's been tangled in that wire," Icy thought with a grin.

He was about to push Snowy into the
fence when he heard a loud 'Baaaa!'

A flock of sheep raced by and knocked
him down.

Snowy didn't notice. He picked some wool
off the fence and walked on.

Snowy entered the wild woods and looked up at the trees. "That twisty branch would make a great walking stick," he said.

Icy climbed the tree behind Snowy. "I'll get you this time, stony face," he thought.

Icy slowly sawed through a heavy
branch. "This will certainly put a
dent in Snowy's hat," he chuckled
to himself.

But the silly snowman had cut
through the branch he was sitting
on. He fell out of the tree and landed
in a prickly holly bush.

Snowy didn't see. He tucked his
branch under his arm and walked on.

"The pebbles around this pond will make great buttons," thought Snowy. Icy tip-toed up behind him.

He went to push Snowy into the pond. But as he did so, Snowy bent over to pick up a pebble.

Icy flew over Snowy,
   slid silently across the icy pond and
   vanished – squelch! – into a patch of reeds.
Snowy put on his new buttons and plodded
back to Emma's house.

He admired his
new stick and pebble
buttons. Then he
mended his scarf.

Meanwhile, Icy
staggered home covered in leaves
and reeds. He was a lumpy mess.

Finally, it was time for the Grand Judging.
Battered Icy came last, while the winner
of the first prize was... Snowy! Emma was
thrilled – although she never did find out
how her clever snowman got his new outfit.

Snow White
and the
Seven Dwarfs

One winter's day, a young Queen stood sewing by her window. As she watched the feathery snowflakes fall, dreaming of the baby she longed to have, her needle slipped.

Three drops of ruby-red blood fell onto the snow. The Queen sighed. "I wish I had a child," she said, "with skin as white as snow, lips as red as blood and hair as black as ebony wood."

Her wish came true.

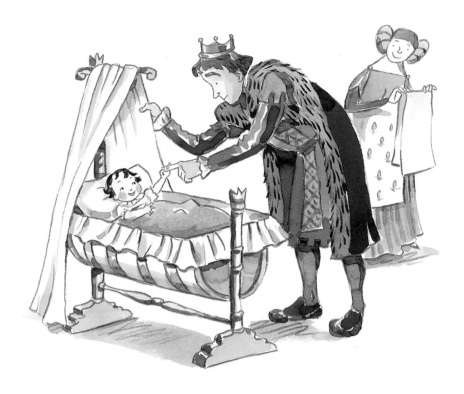

The King was delighted with his newborn daughter and named her Snow White. But his joy was mixed with misery, for in giving birth, the young Queen died.

"My child needs a mother," he thought. Within a year, he had married again.

His new wife was proud and vain. Her heart was so full of love for herself, she had none for anyone else.

The only thing she wanted was to be the most beautiful woman in the world.

Morning and night, she gazed into her magic mirror and asked the same question.

Mirror, mirror on the wall, who's the fairest of us all?

And, morning and night, the mirror replied, "You are, Your Majesty."

The new Queen paid no attention to Snow White, who grew more lovely every day.

Then, one dreadful morning, the Queen asked, "Mirror, mirror on the wall, who's the fairest of us all?" and the mirror said...

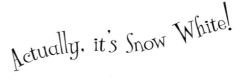

Actually, it's Snow White!

The Queen went pink with rage and her
beautiful face scowled into
the mirror. "I won't have
it," she snarled.

But whenever the Queen asked her
question, the mirror gave the same reply.
The Queen's heart was bursting with
jealousy and she didn't know what to do.

Finally, she could bear it no longer. "Snow White must die!" she decided.

Later that morning, the Queen called for the royal huntsman. "Listen well," she said. "I have a very important job for you."

"Take Snow White to the forest and kill her," she ordered. "I cannot stand her near me for one more second."

Bring me back her lungs and liver, so I know she's dead.

The huntsman was horrified, but he had to obey.

Snow White chatted happily as they went into the forest. The huntsman didn't say a word. Under a giant oak tree, he took out a knife and pulled her from her horse.

"Stop! What are you doing?" she shouted in alarm.

"It's the Queen's orders," said the huntsman sadly. "She wants me to... kill you."

"What?" cried Snow White. "No! Please, let me go," she begged. Her dark eyes filled with tears and the huntsman took pity on her.

As he stood there, he spotted a wild pig in the distance. "I'll take its lungs and liver to the Queen," he thought, "and Snow White will be safe."

He turned to Snow White. "Run, then," he said, "but never return to the palace."

Snow White ran, past
twisty trees and scratchy
brambles. Soon, her black
hair was tangled with leaves.

She ran until the sun started to dip in the sky. Thorny branches like witches' fingers reached out to catch her. Still she ran. She ran until her legs could barely hold her...

...and then she noticed a cottage.
"Maybe someone here can help me," she thought.

To her dismay, there was no one home.
She leaned against the door to catch her
breath and it swung open. Snow White
stumbled inside.

The first thing she
    saw was a tiny table
        and seven tiny chairs.
            Snow White smelled fresh bread
                and honey and her mouth watered.

After so much running, she was starving,
so she sat down and helped herself to bread
and honey. Then she drank every drop of
milk from the seven mugs on the table.

She put down the last mug with a yawn.
Running all day was exhausting. Looking
around, she saw seven tiny beds, each with a
fat feather pillow, standing along one wall.

Snow White tried bed
after bed. The first was too hard.
The second was too narrow... By the time she
reached the seventh bed, she was so tired,
she simply curled up on it anyway.

While Snow White slept, the
cottage door opened and seven dwarfs
trooped in. They each lit a candle and
looked around in surprise.

Who's been in
our cottage?

Who's been
sitting on
my chair?

Who drank
my milk?

Quietly, they gathered around Snow White
and watched her sleeping.

Her skin's as
white as snow.

Her hair's
as black as
ebony.

Her lips are
as red as blood.

"She's beautiful,"
they all sighed together.

Next morning, Snow White was woken by seven songs sung in seven different keys. She jumped out of bed in a panic – but the dwarfs were so friendly, she forgot to be afraid.

When she told them about the Queen, the dwarfs were disgusted. "Stay here," they said. "We'll take care of you."

In her palace bedroom, the Queen was singing too. Smiling at her reflection, she asked her usual question.

Mirror, mirror on the wall, who's the fairest of us all?

"Well, Queen, you are fair, no doubt about it," the mirror said chattily. "But Snow White is fairer. She's living in a cottage in the forest," it added.

"Snow White is alive?" the Queen spat in fury. "That huntsman tricked me!"

She was so angry she couldn't eat or sleep. Instead, she spent every second plotting how to kill Snow White.

At last, she disguised herself as an old pedlar. Packing a basket with ribbons and silks, she set off for the forest.

Snow White was cleaning the cottage when an old woman came to the door.

"Pretty things to sell," the woman cackled. "Silks and satins, belts and bows."

"What lovely silks," cried Snow White, stroking a belt.

"Here, my dear," said the old woman. "Try it on."

She looped the belt around Snow White's waist and pulled it tight... tighter and tighter...

Stop!
Please...

The woman kept pulling until Snow White collapsed.

The dwarfs came home to find Snow White lying in the doorway. Shocked, they saw the belt squeezing the life out of her.

Whipping out a knife, one of the dwarfs sliced through it. Snow White spluttered and began to take deep, shaky breaths.

"Where's the old pedlar woman?" she gasped.

"What old woman?" a dwarf began. "No one knows we're here..." He gave a sudden shout. "Hey! It must have been that wicked Queen. She tricked you."

The dwarfs looked serious.

"You're in grave danger," said one.

"The Queen will keep trying to kill you," said another.

"Don't open the door!" they all said together.

"I won't!" Snow White promised.

Meanwhile, the wicked Queen had run all the way home and raced to her mirror.

Mirror, mirror on the wall, who's the fairest of us all?

Sit down Ma'am...

It's still SnowWhite.

The next day, the Queen was back at the cottage with a poisoned comb. But Snow White refused to let her in.

"You can look, can't you?" said the Queen, holding the sparkling comb to the window.

Snow White was entranced. Forgetting her promise to the dwarfs, she opened the door.

Quicker than a bee, the Queen darted inside and jammed the comb in Snow White's hair. The poison worked at once and she fell to the floor.

As soon as the dwarfs saw Snow White, they knew the Queen had returned.

"Look what she's done now!" said one, taking out the comb.

Snow White moaned. "Oh, my head..."

"You must be more careful," the dwarfs warned her. "The Queen will try again. DON'T open the door!"

Well?

Before you ask, it's still Snow White.

At the palace, the Queen's heart was eaten up with envy. She hated being the second fairest. Angrily, she set to work on her worst spell yet.

In a secret room at the top of the palace, the Queen made a magic apple. It looked so delicious that whoever saw it would have to eat it. But she dipped one half in poison.

Then she dressed up as a farmer's wife and went to the cottage once more.

"I won't buy anything," Snow White called out to her, "and I mustn't open the door."

"I'm not selling," said the Queen quickly. "I just thought you'd like to share this apple."

She held out a shiny red apple. "Mmm, it's deliciously juicy," she added. She took a large bite out of one side and licked her lips. "Here, try it."

"It does look good," agreed Snow White, and took a bite too. That instant, she fell to the ground in a crumpled heap.

153

The Queen laughed. "White as snow, red as blood, black as wood – and dead as dead! At last I'm the most beautiful woman in the world!"

"Not again!" groaned a dwarf, when the dwarfs came home and saw Snow White sprawled on the floor.

But this time, to their great dismay, they couldn't help her.

No belt.

No comb?

I think she's...
dead!

"She's so beautiful," sobbed the youngest dwarf. "We can't bury her." So they laid her in a glass coffin and wrote *The Princess Snow White* upon it.

They placed the coffin on a nearby hill and took turns keeping watch.

Snow White had been there for over a year when a prince rode by. Leaping from his horse, he went up to the coffin.

He saw her skin as white as snow, her lips as red as blood and her hair as black as ebony and he fell in love.

"She's beautiful," he said to the dwarf guarding her. "She's the most beautiful girl I have ever seen."

Please let me take her home with me.

What? No!

"I want to build a splendid tomb for her," the prince explained. "She can't stay on this hillside forever. Besides, a princess belongs in a palace."

The dwarfs argued with the prince all day, but by sunset, they agreed. Almost at once, he was back with four hefty servants to carry the coffin.

But, as they lifted it, one of the men tripped. The coffin jolted and the apple flew from Snow White's mouth. To their astonishment, she opened her eyes.

The prince was overjoyed. He flung open the coffin, swept her up and carried her to his horse.

Where am I?
Who are you?

I'm a prince who wants to marry you!

Back in her palace bedroom, the Queen was heading to her mirror.

"Snow White is the fairest. Ask me another," said the mirror saucily before she could even speak.

With a furious cry, the Queen smashed her mirror into a thousand pieces. And a thousand glass splinters chorused, "Snow White is still the fairest of them all."

Santa's Day Off

"At last," sighed Santa, looking at his calendar. Today was December 26th – his day off.

December
26

After a particularly tiring Christmas, Santa was looking forward to his day of rest.

He snuggled into his softest armchair, with a mug of hot chocolate and a slice of sticky Christmas cake.

As Santa settled down with a big book, two elves burst in.

"We need your help, Santa," wailed Paddy. "We can't get into our house."

"There's a huge polar bear blocking the way," added Pip.

Santa sighed and followed the elves to their home.

A fierce polar bear was pacing up and down outside.

Grrrr!

"If I had some meat, I could lure her away," said Santa.

"There are some sausages in our kitchen," suggested Pip. "If only we could get to them."

Santa had an idea. He crept around the back of the house. Then he climbed up to the chimney and squeezed inside.

Seconds later, he emerged carrying a furry white bundle.

"A polar bear cub!" cried Pip. "He must have climbed in through an open window."

"That's why the mother bear wouldn't let you in," said Santa. "She was protecting him."

The two animals happily plodded off across the snow.

Santa had just settled back in his armchair, when another worried elf rushed in.

"Calm down, Marco," Santa soothed. "What's the matter?"

"We accidentally left someone off this year's list," cried the elf.

Look!

Name: Jason Jeffries

Place: Australia

Would like: A bicycle

Sign below when item has been delivered:

"Get a bike from the store room," said Santa, wearily. "I'll get my sleigh ready."

An hour later, Santa landed at Jason's home.

As Santa carried the bike to the back door, he heard voices.

"Perhaps you'll get your red bike next year, son," said a man.

Santa looked down at the bike. It was blue. He took a deep breath and returned to his sleigh.

One trip to the North Pole later, Santa was back – with a red bike. Jason was overjoyed.
Santa headed north again.

He was almost home, when he heard a cry from below.

"Help! Someone help me!"

Santa went to investigate.

A farmer was standing by a frozen lake.
"My sheep have wandered onto the ice,
Santa," he said. "And it's starting to crack."

Don't let them drown.

Santa flew his sleigh just above the sheep.
"Hover here, boys!" he cried to his reindeer.

Santa gently eased himself over the edge of his sleigh. Reaching down, he grabbed a sheep and lifted it to safety.

Baa!

One by one, he bundled the sheep into his sleigh. The ice finally cracked open just as the last animal left the ice.

Santa returned the sheep to the
grateful farmer.

Santa was exhausted. He returned to his
sleigh and set a course for the North Pole.

When he got home, he staggered into his
living room.

"My hot chocolate will be cold by now," sighed Santa. "And I bet that cake is as dry as dust."

But he was in for a surprise.

How?

On the table by his armchair stood a mug of steaming hot chocolate, a pile of fresh cream cakes and a stack of storybooks.

Even Santa's slippers were warming by
the newly lit fire.

Elves flooded into the room.

Welcome home!

"How kind," smiled Santa.

"Our pleasure, Santa," said Paddy.
"You've shown us that kindness is what
Christmas is all about."

Puss in Boots

Once there was a poor miller, who had three sons. When he died, he left them all he had in the world: his mill, his donkey and his orange tabby cat.

Before anyone could blink, the eldest son took the mill.

Then the middle brother grabbed the
donkey. Tom, the youngest, was left with the
cat. He wasn't impressed.

"You two can work together and earn a
living," Tom grumbled. "What can I do with
Puss? Maybe I'll have to eat him!"

Uh-oh!
I need a plan
and fast.

Later, when they were alone, Puss jumped onto Tom's lap. He pawed at Tom's chest to get his attention.

Don't look so gloomy, Master.

"Things are not as bad as they seem," he said, with a purr. "Just find me a bag, and a pair of leather boots, and you'll see."

Tom was astonished. Puss could talk! He had inherited a *talking* cat.

I have one unbelievably, incredibly amazing cat!

And then Tom remembered that he had often seen Puss using very clever tricks to catch rats and mice.

So, Tom found Puss a large bag and a shiny pair of boots. He gave him a cloak and a floppy hat too.

The cat filled the bag with carrots and strutted off into the fields.

Puss headed for a field where he knew
there were plenty of rabbits. Opening the
bag, he stretched out on the ground and
pretended to be dead.

Just as he expected, a foolish young
rabbit came bouncing along and sniffed the
carrots. As it poked its quivering nose into
the bag, Puss pounced.

Got you!

Puss was delighted with
his catch. He marched
straight to the palace
and asked to see
the king.

In front of the throne, Puss bowed low.
"Your Royal Highness, I have brought you a
gift from my master, the Duke of Carabas."

How amazing!
A talking cat...

"That's kind. Thank your master very
much," replied the king.

The next day, Puss went into
the fields again. This time,
he hid among some
golden corn. He held
his bag wide open...

...and two partridges flew
straight in. Puss chuckled as he pulled the
drawstring tight.

Once more, Puss took his catch to the king.

Take these for your master.

Puss became a regular visitor to the palace. Soon, the king began to wonder who the generous duke was.

One day, Puss took Tom
for a walk by the river.

On his last visit to the palace, Puss had
overheard a guard talking. He knew the king
would be driving past with his beautiful
daughter, Princess Arabella, and he had a plan.

When Puss spotted the royal coach in
the distance, he turned to Tom. "Quick! Take
off your clothes and jump in the river," he
told him.

It's freezing!

Tom was baffled, but he trusted Puss
completely, so he jumped in.

A minute later, Tom was even more puzzled. First, Puss hid all his clothes under a large stone. Then he started to scream.

"Help! Help! Please rescue my master, the Duke of Carabas!"

As the royal coach came by, the king recognized Puss. "Guards! Pull the duke out of the water at once," he commanded.

"Wicked thieves attacked my master and stole all his clothes," Puss explained.

"That's terrible," said the king. "Allow me to help." He snapped his fingers and a servant ran up.

Go to the palace
and fetch some clothes
for the duke.

All this time, Princess Arabella had been watching from the coach.

When she saw Tom in his fine, new clothes, she jumped from her seat. He was so handsome...

Duke of Carabas,
may I introduce my daughter,
Princess Arabella.

Does he
mean me?

Tom bent and kissed Princess Arabella on
the hand.

"Oh!" she gasped, and smiled.

The king insisted that Puss and the duke
join them on their drive.

"You go, master," said Puss, pushing Tom
forward. "I have some errands to run."

Enjoy the drive!
I'll catch up with
you later.

As the coach rumbled along, Puss raced
ahead. He still had lots to do.

Before long, he came to some men mowing a field. Puss clapped his paws.

"Listen to me!" he shouted. "When the king drives by, tell him this field belongs to the Duke of Carabas, or my master will chop you into mincemeat!"

A talking cat — his master must be a magician!

The men didn't dare refuse.

Sure enough, when the king arrived, he asked the men who owned the field.

The Duke of Carabas, Your Highness.

The men had been so frightened by Puss's threats that they all spoke together.

Tom was astonished to hear them tell the king that this was his land, but he decided to play along.

This field always produces a good harvest.

Puss ran ahead. In the next field he passed, some men were reaping grain.

"Tell the king this field belongs to the Duke of Carabas," he snarled, "or my master will grind you into mincemeat!"

Horrified, the men agreed.

When the royal coach arrived at the next
field, the king got out. This field was twice
as big as the one before. "Who owns this
field?" he asked some workers.

"The Duke of Carabas, Your Highness,"
they replied.

Puss made the same threat to everyone
he met. The king was amazed by how much
land the duke owned.

Finally, Puss reached a magnificent castle.

It was owned by a fierce ogre, but that didn't stop Puss.

This ogre happened to be one of the richest ogres in the country. All of the land they had passed on the way actually belonged to him.

The ogre greeted Puss, licking his lips, and invited the cat inside.

Puss smiled. He was about to try his most daring trick. "I have heard," he said to the ogre, "that you can change yourself into any creature you want."

He crossed his paws and frowned. "I'm not sure I believe it. Could you really turn into an elephant or a lion?"

See for yourself!

It was true. In seconds, the ogre turned
into a huge lion. Puss was terrified.

After growling and roaring for a while, the ogre changed back to himself.

"That was the most frightening thing I've ever seen!" cried Puss.

"But I've also been told," he went on, "that you can change into a really small animal, such as a rat or a mouse."

"Of course," said the ogre, rather boastfully.

Surely that's impossible?

Just watch!

211

In a flash, the ogre
transformed. But as soon as
Puss saw the tiny mouse scampering around,
he leaped on him and gobbled him up.

By this time, the royal coach had reached the ogre's castle.

"Go inside," the king ordered his driver. He was curious to see who owned such a grand home.

Puss heard the coach clattering over the drawbridge and flung open the castle doors. "Your Majesty, welcome to the castle of my master, the Duke of Carabas."

"You mean you own this splendid castle, as well as all that land?" the king asked Tom in awe.

Trying to hide his surprise, Tom nodded.

"Would you mind if I took a look around?" asked the king.

"Not at all," said Tom.

In the banqueting hall, a grand feast had been laid out for the ogre. The table was crammed with pies, meat, cheeses, trifles and cakes.

The king's mouth started to water. "That does look good!" he said.

"Please join us for lunch," said Puss.

The king was impressed with the duke's wonderful castle, and Princess Arabella thought he was kind to let them share his feast.

As the king ate, he noticed that the duke and his daughter were getting along very well indeed. He realized the duke would make a perfect prince.

By the end of the meal, the king could not keep his thoughts to himself.

"Duke of Carabas," he declared, "will you marry my daughter?"

If she agrees, I'd be delighted, Sire.

The wedding was arranged for the very next day.

And so the miller's youngest son became a prince and lived happily in the castle with his beautiful bride.

Tom's brothers were both made earls. As for Puss, he became a lord and never had to chase a mouse again...

...except for fun!

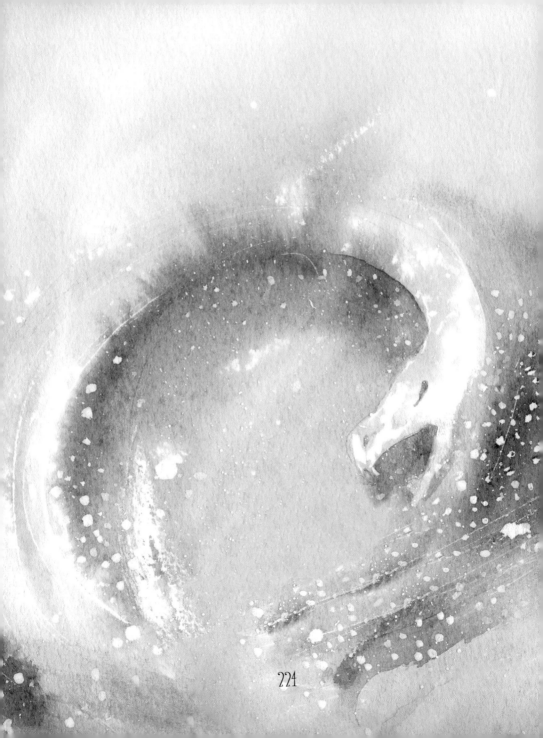

224

The Snow Queen

There was once a wicked demon who created a magic mirror. His mirror made everything good look twisted and ugly.

"It's a fine mirror," growled the demon's students. "Let's show it off to the angels." Flapping their leathery wings, they flew up...

and up...

until...

...the mirror slipped from their hands, crashed to the ground and broke into a million pieces.

smash!

226

Some pieces were no bigger than a grain of sand, but they were as powerful as the whole mirror. If a speck flew into someone's eye, everything looked horrible and wrong.

Worse yet, if a splinter struck a person's heart, that heart began to freeze...

This tale begins not long after the mirror shattered, when splinters of the dangerous glass were still whirling around.

A girl named Gerda was living next door to a boy named Kay. In all the world, no two friends were as close.

One winter's day, as snow was falling, Gerda's grandmother told them the story of the Snow Queen.

"She lives in the icy north, but in winter she flies around, disguised as a snowflake."

"Beware of her!" the grandmother warned. "She's a wicked woman. But don't worry," she added, "if your heart is pure, you'll always see the queen for who she is."

Wandering home that night, Kay gazed
at the sparkling snowflakes drifting
down. As he stared, he noticed one
flake seemed to be growing...

He gasped. The snowflake grew larger...

...until it became a beautiful woman. She was astonishing. Her shimmering white clothes were coated in snow and she herself was made entirely of ice.

The Snow Queen!

The woman turned her cold, bright eyes on Kay. He shook his head and she vanished. "I must have imagined her," he thought.

Winter passed and Kay forgot all about the Snow Queen. Then one day, while he and Gerda watered the roses in her window box, Kay suddenly cried out.

Kay?
What is it?

Ow! My heart!
And my eye!

He had felt a sharp jab in his eye and another, piercing his heart. But neither Kay nor Gerda could see what had happened...

...for the jabs came from splinters of the broken mirror. At once, Kay began to change and grow cruel.

Those roses are ugly!

But Kay! You've always loved them.

Seeing Gerda's frightened face made him angry. Breaking off a handful of roses, he scattered the petals and left. Gerda listened sadly to his boots creaking down the stairs.

After that, Kay saw everything differently. He began to argue and make fun of people in the street. He even mocked Gerda and her roses, though she still loved him.

Next winter, Kay ignored Gerda altogether, and joined the boys on their sleds in the town square.

As they played, a dazzling white sleigh rode into the square. Its driver was dressed in white, from her fur hat to her sharply pointed boots.

Everyone but Kay ran away. He shouted,
"This looks fun!" and tied his sled to the
snow-white sleigh. The two splinters of
mirror had blinded him to danger – for the
driver was none other than the
Snow Queen herself.

Her sleigh picked up speed and Kay
laughed with excitement. It felt like flying.
Hurtling around the square, they dashed out
through the city gates.

On and on they flew, through swirling snow. All too soon, the sleigh stopped. As the driver stood up, Kay realized who she was.

You must be frozen. Come and join me in my sleigh.

The Snow Queen!

Quickly, the queen kissed Kay and his icy heart grew colder. She kissed him again and he forgot all about home. He was trapped.

Back in the town, no one knew where Kay had gone. All through the cold, dead winter, Gerda was too sad to do anything. But when spring came, with no sign of her best friend, she decided to look for him.

"The river flows a long way," she thought. "Perhaps the river has passed him on its travels." Putting on her best, red shoes, she went down to the river.

If I give you my new red shoes, will you take me to Kay?

She threw her shoes into the river as a gift, but they floated back to her. So, she climbed into a boat to throw them further in... and the boat swept her away.

She floated for hours. Gerda was afraid but she couldn't turn back. She hoped the river would take her past someone who had seen Kay. But she saw no one.

As dusk fell, she spotted a rose-covered cottage. The boat began to drift to the bank and an old woman hobbled over.

You poor child!
Are you lost?

The old woman helped Gerda onto the bank and Gerda told her all about Kay. She described their happy days playing until he suddenly changed.

First he grew mean. Then he disappeared altogether.

Now, the old woman wasn't wicked but she did know a little magic – and she lived a lonely life.

"I'll make sure the girl stays with me," she muttered and cast a spell.

To be extra sure, she made all her roses vanish. She didn't want to remind Gerda of the roses at home and her search for Kay.

Eat as many cherries as you like!

Her magic worked. Gerda played happily in the woman's garden and her old life was soon no more real than a dream.

Even so, sometimes she had a feeling that something wasn't quite right.

Gerda might have stayed in the cottage forever but, one day, she spotted a painted flower on the woman's sunhat. It was a rose!

In that moment, Gerda remembered everything. "Kay!" she cried. "How could I forget you? Oh, I've wasted so much time!" Without even saying goodbye to the old woman, she ran away.

Meanwhile, the Snow Queen had taken Kay to her magnificent crystal palace in the far north.

Kay was neither happy nor sad. His feelings were frozen inside him. He sat at the queen's feet, on a vast icy lake, so cold he was almost blue. But he didn't notice.

The queen sat sighing on her throne, bored. Looking down on Kay, she decided to play a game with him. "Solve my puzzle and I'll set you free," she declared.

Kay looked at her blankly.

The queen waved a pale hand at some blocks of ice. "If you put those in the right order, they will spell a word," she said, with a cruel smile.

Slowly, Kay's frozen brain realized she was telling him to spell something. He so wanted to please her but he just couldn't do it.

The Snow Queen laughed. "You'll never do it, my icicle boy!" she said. Her cold laugh bounced off the walls of the castle. "But it's amusing to watch you try..."

Since leaving the cottage, Gerda hadn't stopped running. She simply kept going, with no idea where she was. At last, stumbling through a gloomy forest, she had to rest. Wearily, she sank onto an old tree stump and sighed.

A curious crow hopped up to her, his head to one side. "Caw!" he croaked. "What are you doing, all alone in the world?"

I'm looking for my friend Kay. Have you seen him?

The crow listened to Gerda's story. "Caw, caw..." he said. "I think I might know where he is."

Gerda couldn't believe her luck. "Tell me!" she begged, excitedly.

"Well now," croaked the crow, "there's a princess in this kingdom and she was looking for a prince. In no time at all, men were lining up to meet her. Caawww! But no one was good enough."

"Then a young boy appeared from nowhere. His clothes were torn and his boots creaked. Caawww! But he went inside the palace and – would you believe it – the princess liked him so much, she married him!"

"That must be Kay!" Gerda cried. "He's handsome and clever... and his boots do squeak. Oh, please take me to him!"

"Caw. That might be tricky," said the crow.

"Please help!" Gerda pleaded.

"I'll ask my wife," the crow said at last. "She works in the palace."

The crow flew off and Gerda waited
nervously. Long after sunset, he returned.

"My wife will take you," he croaked.

Trembling with hope, Gerda followed the
crow to the palace. Inside, its grand rooms
were draped in the purple night.

As Gerda crept through the ballroom following the crow's wife, shadowy figures swept by.

"Who are they?" she asked, in a whisper.

"Dreams," replied the crow's wife.

They take the royal thoughts for midnight rides.

In the most splendid room of all, two giant flowers hung from a palm tree. The first flower had pure white petals and, curled up in the middle, lay the princess, fast asleep. The flower beside her was red.

Gerda stepped forward and looked in...

...and the prince woke up. "Who is it?"
he mumbled.

Gerda stared at him and burst into
tears. It wasn't Kay at all.

Gerda's noisy gulps and sobs woke up
the princess.

"Who are you?" she cried. Then, as Gerda
didn't look dangerous, she gave her a hanky
and let her sit down to explain.

That night, Gerda slept in the palace. In the morning, the princess gave Gerda her second-best dress and begged her to stay.

But all Gerda wanted was to search for Kay. "I'll walk around the world if I have to," she said.

The princess smiled and called for her carriage. Gerda gasped. It glistened with golden sugar and inside, the walls were lined with sticky buns and fat cream cakes.

For a second, she simply stared. "Is this really for me?" she asked, pointing to the golden carriage.

"Well, you can hardly walk around the whole world," said the princess, helping her climb in.

Don't worry. I have three more just like it.

The carriage set off and Gerda waved through the window.

"Goodbye! Good luck!" cried the princess.

The carriage rolled up and down hillsides, past villages and towns and winding streams, on and on, until it reached a dark forest. It shone so brightly that it dazzled a band of robbers, who were hiding among the trees.

"Gold!" they shrieked in delight, and rushed to attack.

"Mmm..." said an old robber woman, grabbing Gerda. "She looks tastier than the carriage. Let's eat her!" But, as she raised her knife, something sprang up and bit her on the ear.

You mustn't eat her! I want her!

Ow!

It was the daughter of the chief robber – and she always got her own way.

"I want her for my friend," said the robber girl, pointing to Gerda, "and I want to play with her carriage."

"Hmph," said the old woman grumpily. The little robber girl pushed Gerda into the carriage and squashed in beside her.

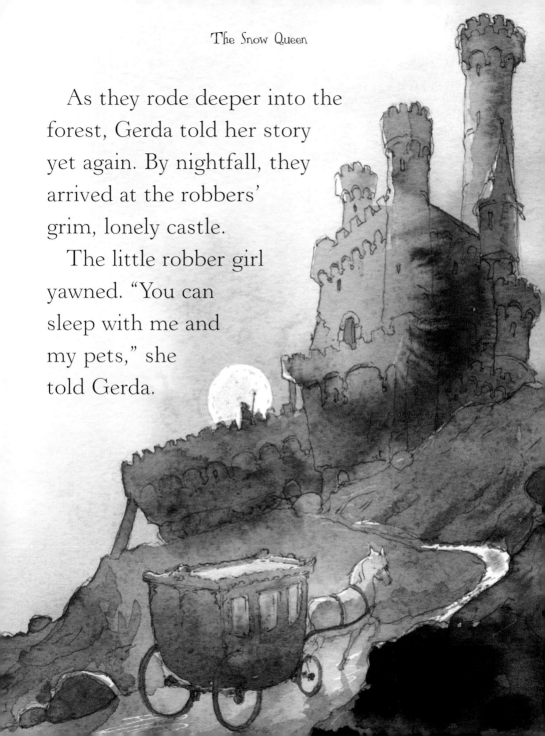

As they rode deeper into the forest, Gerda told her story yet again. By nightfall, they arrived at the robbers' grim, lonely castle.

The little robber girl yawned. "You can sleep with me and my pets," she told Gerda.

Gerda frowned. The robber girl
had very strange pets. One hundred
pigeons roosted in the rafters and
two woodpigeons sat in a silver cage.
"They're all mine!" boasted
the little robber girl. "But Ba is
best of all." And she pointed out a
reindeer, who was tied to the wall.

Say hello,
Ba!

"Bedtime!" she announced suddenly, flopping down. Gerda stayed awake, watching the robbers polish their knives around the fire. Things were worse than ever. She was stuck here, a prisoner once again.

"I'll never find Kay," she sighed. Then the pigeons began talking.

Coo! Did you ever see such a frozen boy?

He'll never thaw now the Snow Queen has him.

"Could the Snow Queen have Kay?" wondered Gerda. "Please, where does the queen live?" she asked the pigeons politely.

"Somewhere north," they cooed. "Ask Ba if he knows."

The reindeer looked up. "Yes," he said, in a slow, deep voice. "I know her home. I'm from there too."

She lives in the far, far north, past Lapland.

The little robber girl, who was still awake, heard everything.

"You don't want to find that rotten old Snow Queen," she said at once. "You'd be safer here with us." But Gerda was desperate to find Kay.

"Then I shall let you go," said the robber girl, as proudly as a queen herself. "Ba shall take you."

"You'll need food," she added, finding Gerda some bread and ham. With a hard shove, she helped Gerda on to the reindeer's silky-smooth back.

Ba bounded off happily, racing north to his home. The little robber girl stood alone in the moonlight, watching and waving until they were out of sight.

It was a long way to Lapland, their first stop on the way to the Snow Queen's palace. When they arrived, Ba and Gerda were spotted by a Lapp woman.

"You're frozen!" she exclaimed to Gerda, taking them into her hut. "And you've many a mile to go yet," she went on, when she heard their tale.

"Still, you're in luck," she said. "The Snow Queen is away just now, creating the Northern Lights. From here, you must go on to Finmark. I know a Finn woman who can help."

Gerda watched in surprise as the woman quickly scribbled a message to her friend on a dried fish.

Ba galloped off once more across the snowy plains, until they reached the Finn woman's tiny hut.

First, the Finn woman read the fish. Then she listened as Gerda breathlessly told her tale. Nodding, she fetched a parchment from her shelves and studied it.

Finally, she took Ba aside. "Kay *is* with the Snow Queen," she whispered. "He's under her spell, because of splinters of glass in his eye and his heart. To rescue him, Gerda must get the splinters out."

"But how?" growled Ba. "Can you give her some magic?"

"Gerda has come this far," the Finn woman said. "She is good and sweet and innocent. That will be all the magic she needs."

"Take Gerda as far as the Snow Queen's garden," she added in a low voice. "But don't tell her what I've told you." She swept Gerda up and placed her on the reindeer's back.

Go quickly now!

Goodbye! And thank you.

Ba galloped until they reached a bush with glossy red berries. There, he stopped and let Gerda down.

Gerda was left all alone in the icy cold. Glittering snowflakes whirled around, making it difficult for her to move. They were the guards of the Snow Queen's castle.

As she hesitated, the guards took on terrible shapes. Huge hedgehogs with vicious spikes, fang-toothed snakes and fierce bears all sprang at her. Gerda cried out in fear, but she didn't run away.

Standing boldly before the guards, she told them to leave her alone. Her breath blew out in misty clouds around her. To her astonishment, these clouds became angels, who began to attack the guards.

Seeing the angels gave Gerda strength. She punched the bear nearest to her and he melted at her touch. Then the angels warmed Gerda's icy feet and hands and she hurried into the castle.

Inside a cold, empty hall, Kay was puzzling over the Snow Queen's challenge. He sat still, thinking hard... so still that he seemed frozen stiff. And that was how Gerda found him, when she appeared moments later.

"Kay!" she called, running up to him. She wrapped her arms around him, but he didn't move.

Gerda didn't know what to do. It was like hugging a block of ice. He didn't even look at her.

Hot tears ran down her face and dripped off her nose onto Kay's chest. They reached right through to his heart, thawing the ice and washing away the splinter of glass.

Kay seemed to soften, so Gerda started to talk about the roses back home. Her words and his melting heart brought tears to Kay's eyes too... tears which washed away the splinter there.

At long last, he could see clearly again. "Gerda!" he shouted. "Is it really you?" The old Kay was back.

Gerda and Kay laughed and cried and jumped for joy. Even the blocks of ice around them got up and danced. When the blocks fell down again, they spelled the word *Eternity*. Kay was free.

Gerda kissed and kissed his cheeks so that they glowed.

"Gerda! Yuck!" said Kay, but Gerda kept kissing him until he was completely thawed.

"Let's go!" begged Kay. "The Snow Queen could be back at any minute..."

"She's back now!" said an icy voice, behind them.

Kay and Gerda looked at each other in horror.

"You said if I spelled a word I was free," Kay shouted bravely, "and there it is! So I'm going!"

The Snow Queen was furious but there was nothing she could do. She had given her word and she was bound by it.

Laughing with relief, Gerda and Kay tore outside the castle, to find Ba waiting for them. To Gerda's delight, the reindeer carried them all the way home.

Finally, they arrived at Gerda's house. Her grandmother had given up hope of ever seeing either of them again.

Is it really you? You defeated the Snow Queen?

Gerda and Kay hugged the grandmother over and over.

"This is truly a fairy-tale ending!" cried the grandmother and the roses in the window box nodded their heads, as if to agree.

286

East of the Sun, West of the Moon

Far away to the north, where the land is covered in thick, dark forests and the wind blows bitterly cold, there lived a poor family.

Late one snowy afternoon, they sat huddled around the hearth, warming their hands by the fire.

The boys were handsome, the girls pretty – but the youngest, Asta, was the most beautiful of all.

As dusk began to close in around the cottage, there came a knock at the door. "Who's there?" called the father. But there was no answer. So the father rose and opened the door.

There was a rush of icy cold air... and before him stood a towering white bear.

"I have watched your family all summer," said the bear, in a rumbling voice. "And I am ready to make you an offer."

"If you give me your youngest daughter," he went on, "I can make you as rich as you are now poor."

"I'll not give you my daughter," said the father, blocking the way, "however poor we may be."

But Asta looked into the sad, black eyes of the great white bear, and made up her mind.

"We barely have enough food to eat," she said. "And our clothes are turning to rags. How will we survive the winter? I will go with the bear."

So saying, she stood up, collected a small bundle of belongings and walked steadily to the door.

"Don't go!" cried her mother.

"The bear must be under a spell," she whispered in her daughter's ear.

"Don't worry, Mother," said Asta, "I am not afraid."

Asta climbed on the bear's back.

"Keep a tight hold of my fur," he told her.
Then, before anyone could stop him, he
bounded away into the night.

While the moon was still high in the
sky, Asta and the bear arrived at a craggy
black mountain.

The bear raised his huge paw and knocked on the mountainside. A door creaked open...

Inside, was a glittering castle, carved from stone.

The white bear handed Asta a golden bell.
"Ring this if you need anything," he said.

No sooner had Asta taken the bell, than
she found herself alone in a grand bedroom.
She lay down on the bed, but couldn't sleep.

Clouds passed over the moon, sinking the castle into darkness. Footsteps echoed down the corridor. Asta peered out from her room, and saw a man in the shadows.

He dragged behind him a white bear skin, which gleamed in the moonlight.

Each night after that, Asta watched the
man wander the corridors. "Is that the bear,
changed into a man?" she wondered.
She longed to see his face.

The days rolled on. Asta had everything she could ask for. And, each evening, the bear would come and sit by her side. She would stroke his soft fur and sing to him.

The bear would rest his head on her lap, with a glimmer of hope in his dark eyes.

But Asta felt lonely in the castle, with the bear who rarely spoke. All day she would sit and wonder about the man who walked in the shadows.

The white bear watched the roses fade from her cheeks. "What is it?" he asked one day. "What do you want?"

"I want to go home – just for one day."

"That can be arranged," said the white bear. "If you will only promise me not to talk to your mother alone."

They set out the next day, with Asta astride the white bear's back. At last they came to a large farmhouse. "This is where your family lives now," said the bear.

"I will leave you for a night and a day. But don't forget what I said, or you will do much harm to us both."

I'll remember, I promise.

Asta was filled with happiness to see her family again. But before she left, her mother managed to get her alone.

Asta soon told her about the man who paced the corridors at night – and how she'd never seen his face.

"You might be living with a troll!" her mother said. "Take this candle. Hide it in your clothes and light it when he's asleep."

That night, Asta kindled her light, then
followed the man to his room. She held
it above his sleeping form, and saw the
handsomest prince of her dreams.

Unable to resist, she bent down and kissed
his cheek. As she did so, three hot drops of
wax fell upon his shirt.

The prince woke with a start. "What have you done?" he cried. "I've been bewitched by the troll queen, so I'm a bear by day and a man by night."

"I was to be set free if I could find a girl who would love me for a year... without seeing my human face."

"Now I must go to the castle
that lies east of the sun and west
of the moon." He shuddered. "And
there I must marry the troll queen."

"Can't I go with you?" Asta begged.
"No," answered the prince.

"The troll queen has me
under a powerful spell.
I must go to her."

"Then I'll follow you there," vowed Asta.
"You can try," said the prince sadly, "but
you'll never find me."

When Asta awoke the next morning, both
the prince and the castle had gone.

She was lying in a forest clearing, with nothing but the clothes she came in. "I'll head north," Asta decided, "because that is where the trolls dwell."

Asta walked for many days and many nights, until her feet were sore and her legs were weary.

She thought of her last journey on the white bear's back – the feel of his thick, soft fur and the speed at which he bounded along.

"I'll never find him," she wept.

"You shouldn't give up so easily," croaked a voice. Asta looked up to see an old woman.

"Can you help me?" she asked, eagerly. "I'm looking for my prince. He's in the castle that lies east of the sun and west of the moon."

"Aha!" said the old woman. "So you're the girl. I've heard tales of you and your search."

I can help you.

"I'll give you my horse and three golden gifts," she went on.

She handed Asta a comb, an apple and a pear. "To find the castle, ride until you meet the East Wind," the old woman said. "That is all I know."

Asta climbed on the horse's back and the old woman whispered in its ear. A moment later, they were off.

"Thank you!" called Asta, as her voice was whipped away by the wind.

The horse's hooves pounded over the
ground. Faster and faster he flew and Asta
clung to his mane.

On a cliff top overlooking a rolling sea,
the horse finally came to a stop. All around
them, the East Wind blew in gentle gusts.

"I'm looking for the castle that lies east of
the sun and west of the moon," Asta told him.

318

"I have never blown that far," the East Wind replied. "I will take you to my brother, the West Wind. He may know the way, for he is stronger than I."

Asta climbed on the East Wind's back and they roared away over the waves, to the land where the West Wind lived.

"Brother," called the East Wind, "do you know the way to the castle that lies east of the sun and west of the moon?"

"No," said the West Wind. "I have never blown that far. But I will take the girl to the South Wind, for he is much stronger than either of us and has roamed far and wide."

So they rode to the land where the South Wind lived.

"Only the North Wind knows the way to the castle," said the South Wind, "for he is the oldest and strongest of us all. I will carry you there."

When they came near the North Wind, Asta felt his presence in the frantic, icy blasts of air.

"What do you want?" he roared.

"I carry the one who seeks the prince, in the castle east of the sun and west of the moon," the South Wind replied.

"I know it," said the North Wind. "I blew there once, but I was so tired that for many days after, I could not blow at all."

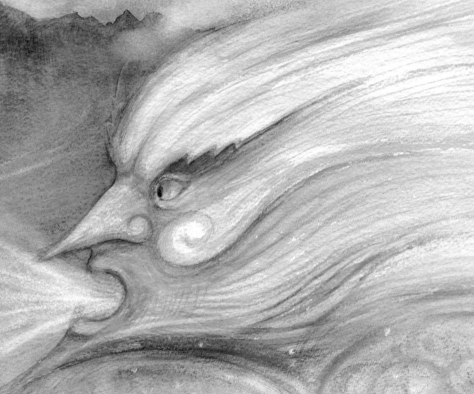

"If you are not afraid to go with me," the North Wind went on, "I will take you there."

Asta thought of her prince
with his sad, black eyes.
"I am not afraid,"
she said.

The North Wind puffed himself up until he was so huge and strong, he was terrible to see. Asta climbed on his back and together they flew through the air.

Below them, storms raged over the oceans and ships were tossed like toys on the roaring waves.

They blew so far that even the North
Wind felt tired. He sank lower and lower,
until the waves dashed against Asta's feet.
"Nearly... there..." he puffed, and
with a final gust, he laid Asta
down on an icy shore.

Above her, east of the sun
and west of the moon, rose
the troll queen's castle.
Exhausted, Asta crawled
into a cave, and slept.

Asta woke from her sleep to find
herself covered in frost.

With stiff limbs, she climbed the crags
to the castle door. From behind a rock, she
watched the trolls lumbering in and out.

They carried buckets and mops, rolls of
red carpet and yards of white silk.

"They're preparing for the wedding!" Asta gasped, and she slipped inside the castle to search for her prince.

Finally, she came to a grand room lit by candlelight. There, on a great stone throne, sat the troll queen herself.

She had string-like hair which she combed with long, yellow nails, and a nose that drooped down to her lap.

"What do you want?" she
asked, in a voice like
grinding stones.
"I've come to see the
prince," Asta replied.

The troll queen beckoned Asta closer.
"First you must give me something in
return," she said.

Asta looked down at her tattered clothes, then remembered the old woman's gifts. "I could give you this golden comb?" she said.

The troll queen grabbed it from her with a claw-like hand. "You may see the prince tonight," she snapped. "He's in the room at the top of the tallest tower."

That night, Asta rushed to the prince's room, and there she found him, fast asleep. She shook him and called to him but nothing would wake him.

In the morning, the troll queen returned. "Now get out of my castle!" she cried.

Asta spent the day in her
cave. As evening drew in,
she stood beneath the troll
queen's window, playing
with her golden apple.

"Give it to me!"
the troll queen called.
"What will you give me in
return?" Asta asked.

335

"You may visit the prince tonight," the troll queen replied.

But again there was no waking him. And, as soon as morning came, she was dragged from the castle by the troll queen's guards.

With one last gift to use, Asta stood
beneath the troll queen's window once more.
Her golden pear glinted
in the pale light of the
northern sun.

"You may see the prince tonight,"
gloated the troll queen, "in return for that
shining pear."

"But it'll be the last time," she added, "for tomorrow we marry and then he'll be mine."

That night, like the others, the prince slept like one enchanted. Then it came to Asta how she might break the spell.

Hidden within the folds of her clothes, was the candle her mother had given her so long ago. She lit it and watched three drops of hot wax fall onto the sleeping prince...

With a start, he woke.

"You've come just in time," the prince cried. "I was to marry the troll queen tomorrow night, but you've found me before the year is out."

Then, from the stone turret, came the sound of heavy feet.

"We must flee," urged Asta. "The troll queen is coming."

As she spoke, the first light of dawn pricked the night sky.

"I am still a bear for one
more day," roared
the prince.

Turning, Asta saw
he was a white bear once more.
"Climb on my back," he said.

As the troll queen opened the bedroom door, the bear charged past her down the turret stairs.

"Come back!" she cried.

"Never," snarled the bear.

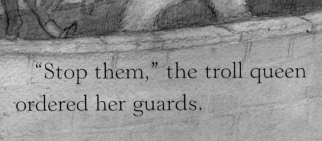

"Stop them," the troll queen ordered her guards.

But the trolls were no match for the
giant bear. With one swipe from his paw
he scattered them like leaves, then burst
through the castle door.

Together, Asta and the bear galloped to the
icy shore. There, a boat bobbed on the water.
In one bound, the bear leaped aboard.

"I thought you would need help escaping," said the North Wind. "All this time I have been resting. Now I will take you home."

For months, they journeyed south, the North Wind blowing them across the ocean as gently as he could.

"I have lost my riches," the prince told Asta. "All my treasure is trapped in the troll queen's castle."

"She can keep it!" laughed Asta. "I know of a beautiful farmhouse where we can live..."

When at last they stepped off the boat, Asta turned to the North Wind and asked, "Why did you and your brother winds help me?"

"Your story was foretold to us," the North Wind replied. "For you are the girl who went to the ends of the earth for love."

About the Authors

Hans Christian Andersen (1805-1875)

Hans Christian Andersen was born in Denmark in 1805, the son of a poor shoemaker, and had a passion for storytelling from an early age. He left home at fourteen and moved to Copenhagen to seek his fortune. After a short time as an actor, he turned to writing.

He produced his greatest works in his mid-twenties – many of them fairy tales, including such classics as *The Twelve Dancing Princesses*, *The Little Mermaid* and *The Emperor's New Clothes* – and became a well-known literary figure across Europe. His stories have been popular with children and adults alike ever since.

Charles Dickens (1812–1870)

Charles Dickens was a Victorian writer who lived in London. When he was twelve, he was sent to work in a factory. He hated it and never forgot how hard life could be for the poor.

His novels often highlighted the harshness of life in Victorian England and the huge gap between the wealthy and those who had nothing.

In 1843, he began a series of stories known as the Christmas books, which he wrote over the next five years. These included *The Chimes*, *The Cricket on the Hearth*, *The Battle of Life* and *The Haunted Man*. But the first one he wrote was *A Christmas Carol* and it remains the most famous.

The Brothers Grimm
Jacob (1785-1863) & Wilhelm (1786-1859)

Jacob and Wilhelm Grimm were brothers who lived in Germany. When they grew up they became librarians and professors, studying German folk tales and the German language. In 1812, they published the book *Children's and Household Tales*, which included the tales *Cinderella, Hansel and Gretel, Rapunzel* and *Rumpelstiltskin*.

Clement Clarke Moore (1779-1863)

Clement Clarke Moore was an American Professor of Classics who lived in New York, USA. He is thought to have written *A Visit from Saint Nicholas* in 1822 as a Christmas present for his children.

Charles Perrault (1628–1703)

Charles Perrault lived in France in the 1600s, and studied law before working for the government. In 1695, he lost his job and decided to concentrate on writing. His book *Stories, or Tales from Times Past, with Morals* was published in 1697 and included the now famous fairy tales, *Cinderella*, *Sleeping Beauty*, *Little Red Riding Hood* and *Puss in Boots*. These he developed from existing folk tales.

Russell Punter (1965–)

Russell Punter was born in Bedfordshire, England. When he was young, he enjoyed making up and illustrating his own stories. His ambition as a boy was to become a cartoonist.

When he grew up, he studied art at college, before becoming a graphic designer and writer. He has written over twenty children's books to date.

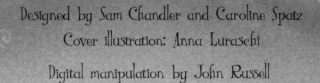

Designed by Sam Chandler and Caroline Spatz
Cover illustration: Anna Luraschi

Digital manipulation by John Russell

First published in 2009 by Usborne Publishing Ltd, 83-85 Saffron Hill,
London EC1N 8RT, England.
www.usborne.com Copyright © 2009 Usborne Publishing Ltd.
The name Usborne and the devices 🎈 🏠 are Trade Marks of Usborne Publishing Ltd.

All rights reserved. No part of this publication may be reproduced, stored in a retrieval system,
or transmitted in any form or by any means, electronic, mechanical, photocopying,
recording or otherwise, without the prior permission of the publisher.

First published in America in 2010. UE.